Twisted Candy Apples

STEPHANIE SWANN

Contents

Dedication

To everyone who feels different, awkward, weird... you are beautiful and you do deserve love.

1: Elijah

The Halloween fair buzzed with life, as vibrant colors and festive decorations adorned the stalls and walkways. Strings of twinkling orange lights danced in the soft autumn breeze, casting a warm glow on the patrons below. Jack-o'-lanterns grinned mischievously from every corner. The enticing scent of caramel and cinnamon wafted through the air, drawing me deeper into the heart of the celebration.

"Excuse me," I chuckled as I gently nudged my way through the throng of people, already feeling the pull of the delicious aromas that beckoned to me.

As I continued to weave my way through the fair, I felt a sense of belonging. Surrounded by laughter and merriment, I was right at home amidst the chaos. My charming personality often drew others to me, and tonight was no exception. Strangers easily struck up conversations, and I engaged in lighthearted banter with fellow fairgoers.

"Have you tried the caramel apples yet?" asked a woman dressed as a witch, her eyes sparkling beneath the brim of her pointed hat.

"No, not yet! But I can't wait to get my hands on one," I replied, my mouth watering at the thought.

"Trust me, they're to die for!" she cackled before disappearing into the crowd.

"Thanks for the tip!" I called after her.

My eager steps led me directly to a stand that seemed to be the source of the tantalizing aromas swirling around the fair. The scent of caramel and cinnamon was nearly irresistible, drawing me in like an invisible hand.

"Hi there!" I greeted the strikingly handsome man behind the counter, his intense focus on arranging the tower of candy apples momentarily broken by my presence. "These smell amazing!"

"Thank you," he replied shyly, a hint of a smile playing on his lips as he looked up to meet my eyes. There was something incredibly endearing about his shyness.

"Can I have one, please?" I asked, unable to resist reaching for the nearest candy apple. As I did so my enthusiasm got the better of me, and I accidentally bumped into him, causing our hands to collide and the candy apples to stick together in a gooey mess.

"Oops! I'm so sorry!" I exclaimed, feeling my cheeks heat up with embarrassment. "I didn't mean to cause any trouble."

He looked at the sticky mess with wide eyes before letting out a soft chuckle. "It's alright, accidents happen," he said.

We both tugged gently at the stubborn treats, and it soon became clear that we were only making the mess worse. Our eyes met, and we burst into laughter.

"Looks like we're really in a sticky situation here," I joked.

"Indeed, we are," he agreed, grinning. His smile was captivating, and I wanted to see it more often.

"Maybe we should just leave them like this – a new invention, 'candy apple clusters,'" I suggested.

"Or a lesson on how not to make candy apples," he added, his eyes twinkling with amusement.

As we shared that moment of laughter, something clicked between us. It felt like I had known him for years, yet we had just met. The connection was undeniable, and a wave of warmth washed over me. His whole persona was appealing.

"Tell you what," I said, still chuckling, "how about I buy these two stuck-together apples as well? Consider it my apology for causing this mess in the first place."

His eyes widened in surprise before he shook his head. "You really don't have to—"

"Please," I interrupted, "I insist."

"Alright, if you're sure," he conceded, gracing me with another one of those enchanting smiles.

"Thanks," I replied sheepishly. As I watched him carefully select a new candy apple for me, I realized I didn't want the conversation to end. I wanted more. More of him. More candy apples. More. "I'm Elijah, by the way."

"Nice to meet you, Elijah," he responded softly, handing me the new candy apple with a warm smile. "I'm Ronan."

"Ronan," I repeated, savoring the sound of his name on my lips. "I like it."

"Thank you," he said, his cheeks flushing a charming shade of pink.

After I handed him the money, he turned to tend another customer, but I quickly interjected.

"Ronan, I have to ask," I began, leaning against the stand as I tried to continue our conversation. "How did you get into candy making?"

He glanced over at me with a bashful smile, clearly not used to talking about himself. "Well, honestly, it started when I was a kid. My mom taught me some basic recipes, and I just fell in love with the process."

"Your mom, huh?" I mused. "So, is this a family business?"

"Sort of," Ronan admitted, rubbing the back of his neck. "My mom always made candy for special occasions, but she never sold them or anything. I decided to turn her passion into something more when I got older. That's when I started this stand."

"Wow," I breathed, genuinely impressed. "That's quite the tribute to your mom."

"Thanks," he said, his cheeks reddening slightly. "I like to think she'd be proud of what I've accomplished."

"I'm sure she would be," I offered reassuringly. "And speaking of accomplishments, I've noticed you've got some unique flavors here. How do you come up with these ideas?"

"Trial and error, mostly," Ronan explained, gesturing to the assortment of confections on display. "I'm always trying out new combinations and techniques. Some work better than others, but I enjoy the experimentation."

"Amazing," I said, my eyes scanning the various candies. "You know, I've got a sweet tooth myself, but I've never been much of a cook." I chuckled, remembering my many kitchen disasters. "But candy... there's just something magical about it, isn't there?"

"Definitely," Ronan agreed. "It can transport you to another world filled with joy and wonder."

"Exactly!" I exclaimed, excited that someone else understood my fascination with sweets. "It's like each piece is a little burst of happiness, just waiting to be shared."

"Couldn't have said it better myself," he smiled softly, and I felt that familiar warmth in my chest again.

We spent the better part of an hour talking about everything from our favorite candies to the most challenging recipes we'd ever attempted. Ronan's eyes sparkled with excitement when he spoke about his craft, and I was drawn to his passion and dedication. And despite his initial shyness, he seemed to open up more and more as the evening wore on, growing comfortable with me.

"Alright, I've got one more question for you," I teased playfully. "What's your favorite candy?"

Ronan thought for a moment before responding with a shy grin. "That's a tough one, but I think I'd have to say... chocolate-covered strawberries and candy canes."

"Really?" I asked, surprised by his choice. "I would've thought it'd be something more, well, fancy."

"Sometimes the simplest things are the best," he replied with a shrug.

"True," I conceded, smiling back at him. "Well, I can certainly agree with that sentiment."

The balance between my outgoing nature and Ronan's quiet charm created an atmosphere of ease and understanding. It was clear to me that this chance meeting at the fair was the start of something truly special. At some point he'd been so caught up in our conversation he decided just to close his stand and walk with me.

"Come on, let's try some of these games," I suggested to Ronan as we wandered through the bustling Halloween fair. The night sky, dotted with twinkling stars, provided a picturesque backdrop for the brightly lit stalls and the laughter of children.

"Alright, but I should warn you—I'm not exactly the most skilled at these things," Ronan admitted, rubbing the back of his neck.

"Hey, no worries! It's all in good fun," I assured him, giving him a reassuring pat on the shoulder. As we approached the game booths, I noticed a ring-toss set up with various prizes displayed. "How about this one?"

"Sure, why not?" Ronan agreed hesitantly, his eyes flicking to the prizes—adorable plush toys dressed as classic Halloween characters. A mischievous grin spread across my face as I handed over our tickets to the attendant and picked up three rings each.

"Alright, let's see who has better aim, shall we?" I challenged, taking a step back and tossing my first ring. It sailed through the air, landing squarely around a bottle. I pumped my fist in the air triumphantly before smirking at Ronan. "Your turn!"

"Beginner's luck," Ronan mumbled, rolling his eyes at my antics. He took a deep breath, closed one eye, and carefully flung his first ring. To both of our surprise, it hooked perfectly.

"Nice shot!" I exclaimed, clapping him on the back. Our laughter mingled as we continued to compete, each victory more exhilarating than the last. The shared joy of playing these simple games brought us an easy way to get to know each other.

"Alright, let's take a break and try some treats," I suggested, my gaze drifting toward a nearby stall offering fresh funnel cakes. Ronan's eyes lit up as we walked over at the sight of the mouthwatering goods. We purchased a warm funnel cake, drizzled generously with powdered sugar, and found a cozy bench to share it on.

"Ronan, do you ever think about how much happiness your candy creations bring to people?" I asked, taking a bite of the sweet, fried dough.

"Sometimes," he admitted, his cheeks flushing slightly as he chewed thoughtfully. "It's a wonderful feeling when someone enjoys something you've made with your own hands."

We ate in silence for a few moments before continuing our walk.

"Wow, look at that!" Ronan exclaimed as we stopped by a stall selling intricate, handmade candles. The delicate wax figures seemed to come alive with each flickering flame, dancing an eternal waltz of light and shadow.

"Beautiful, isn't it?" I mused. "The way they've captured the essence of motion...it's like watching magic."

"Exactly," he agreed, his eyes reflecting the candlelight with a softness that reached deep into my soul. We shared a smile.

"Hey, do you want to try the Ferris wheel?" I suggested, stealing a quick glance at the towering ride. The colorful lights adorning the structure flickered, casting a gentle glow on Ronan's face.

"Sure." His voice trembled slightly, and I could sense a hint of nervousness behind his shy smile. My chest swelled with protectiveness for this introverted candy maker who had unknowingly captured my attention.

"Come on, then." I grabbed his hand and squeezed lightly, guiding us toward the line for the Ferris wheel. As we waited, I felt the subtle brush of his shoulder against mine, a silent gesture of gratitude for my unwavering presence.

"Two tickets, please," I said to the attendant, handing over the money. We climbed into the gondola, anticipation bubbling within me as the ride began its slow ascent.

"Wow," Ronan breathed, his gaze sweeping across the fairgrounds below. The vibrant colors of the stalls and games melded into a kaleidoscope of life, painting a breathtaking scene beneath us.

"Amazing," I agreed, my heart swelling with the beauty of the moment. As we reached the peak of the Ferris wheel, time slowed, allowing us to savor the intimacy of this moment.

"Thank you, Elijah," Ronan whispered. "For tonight... I... I haven't felt this way in a long time."

"Thank you, too." I responded. "I haven't either."

As we descended from the heights, I knew that the evening was ending, yet the magic between Ronan and me remained untouched by time. The anticipation of what lay ahead for us lingered in the air.

"Let's make a promise," I suggested, the words slipping out before I could stop them. "No matter what the future holds, we'll remember this night—the beginning of something special between us." It was a bold move. Asking a stranger to make me a promise, but I needed to know he held a small space for me in his heart, too.

"Promise," Ronan murmured, his eyes shining with sincerity as our fingers tightened around one another, sealing the vow between us.

The last strains of laughter from the fairgoers below floated up to us as the Ferris wheel made its final rotation. Fairgoers had started to head home, but I wanted this to last. I felt Ronan's hand linger in mine, our fingers entwined like the ribbons of an intricate candy twist.

"Time flies when you're having fun," I mused, my eyes drawn to the crescent moon illuminating the sky. "But this night...it feels like it will last forever."

"Me too," Ronan agreed, his voice soft and tinged with wonder.

As we stepped off the Ferris wheel and onto solid ground, we were enveloped by the scent of caramel and cinnamon – a tangible reminder of the passion that brought us together. The fair was almost empty. But the world beyond the fairgrounds seemed so distant, almost irrelevant, as our connection held us captive.

"Shall we walk back to your stand?" I asked, glancing at Ronan with a playful grin. "We might have some candy apples to salvage after all."

"Sounds like a plan," he smiled back, his cheeks still flushed from the excitement of the evening.

We wandered through the stragglers, our laughter mingling with the final echoes of delight from children clutching stuffed animals won at various games. As we reached Ronan's stand, I couldn't help but feel a pang of sadness that our magical night was drawing to a close. Yet, deep within me, an ember of hope began to take root, fueled by the promise we'd made atop the Ferris wheel.

"Before we say goodnight," I said, turning to face him, "I just want you to know how much this night meant to me." I hesitated, my heart pounding in my chest. "And that I want to get to know you better. Maybe take you out sometime."

"Thank you, Elijah," Ronan replied, his eyes meeting mine with a warmth that seemed to chase away the autumn chill. "I feel the same way."

We stood there, our hands still joined, as the last remnants of the Halloween fair faded around us. The vibrant colors, festive decorations, and enticing aromas now mere memories that would linger long after we'd parted ways.

"Until next time?" I asked, raising an eyebrow in hopeful anticipation.

"Definitely," he answered, slipping his business card into my free hand.

2: Ronan

The town's Halloween market shimmered with a festive atmosphere as the coordinator hung the last of the orange lights. The market was alive with laughter and the rustling of fallen leaves underfoot while children darted between stalls, playing tag.

"Look at those caramel apples, Ronan!" Elijah exclaimed, his hair catching the flickering light of a nearby lantern. His contagious smile shone as bright as the decorations around us, and I couldn't help but feel swept up in the excitement. "We should try them. I know they won't be as good as yours, but..." He trailed off. This was our fourth date this week, and he seemed too good to be true. He was literally perfect in every way. And I was... well, me. Awkward. Weird.

"Sure," I agreed, my voice barely above a whisper. With each step we took together, my heart raced a little faster. I wondered if he could feel the nervous energy radiating off me as we continued our journey through the market.

"Tell me something," Elijah said, "what's your favorite Halloween memory?"

I hesitated, searching my mind for an answer while trying to keep my composure. "I-I'm not sure. I've loved making candy for people to enjoy, though."

"Aw, that's so sweet," Elijah replied, gently squeezing my hand. "You really do have a gift, you know. Your passion shines through in everything you make."

"Thank you," I murmured, feeling my cheeks warm under the weight of his compliment. As we walked, I couldn't shake the sense that something important was about to happen between us. The magical ambiance of the Halloween market seemed to amplify the deep connection we'd been building, and I wasn't sure how much longer I could keep my emotions in check.

"Let's sit down for a moment," Elijah suggested, gesturing towards a nearby bench nestled among the pumpkins and hay bales.

"Okay," I agreed. And so, we took our place on the bench, our hands still clasped together, as the magic of Halloween swirled around us.

Sitting on the bench, surrounded by flickering jack-o'-lanterns and pumpkin spice wafting through the air, I felt the same rush of child-like wonder I always got this time of year. Except this year, it felt better than years past. It was as if the world had conspired to create this perfect moment for Elijah and me.

"Ronan," Elijah said softly, his voice laced with uncertainty, "I want to tell you something."

"Of course," I replied. "You can share anything with me."

He took a deep breath. "In the past, I've only ever dated women. But when I'm with you... it's different, you know? I've never felt this way about another man before, and it's confusing, but also... thrilling."

My eyes widened, surprised by his honesty. I could feel the warmth of his hand still holding mine, anchoring us together in this moment of shared vulnerability. "Elijah, I appreciate you telling me that. I'm glad you trust me enough to share your feelings." Truth was, I was conflicted. I'd never dated anyone, and he'd never dated men. How on earth could we navigate this? I'd expected that he would at least have some kind of experience.

"Of course, I trust you," he smiled, his eyes meeting mine. "You're kind, caring, and incredibly talented. You deserve to know."

"Thank you," I whispered, feeling the weight of the words as they hung in the cool autumn air.

I wanted to end the conversation there; this was... hard for me. Hard to open up, but he deserved to know.

"Actually, Elijah," I began hesitantly, "I've had my own struggles when it comes to understanding my emotions and navigating relationships. I haven't really dated much, or at all." I looked down. How embarrassing.

The words tumbled out of me, revealing a vulnerability I hadn't shared with many people before. The crisp autumn breeze rustled the fallen leaves around us, as if encouraging me to continue.

"Really?" Elijah asked, his eyes full of empathy.

"Yeah," I confessed, feeling a strange mix of relief and anxiety. "I find it difficult to know what I'm feeling or how to express it, and that's made dating even more complicated."

"Thank you for telling me," Elijah said. "It means a lot that we can share this with each other."

As we sat in contemplation, I noticed children with sticky faces and hands having the time of their lives, while unhurried parents followed behind them, deep in conversations. I wanted that. I wanted this... with him. Oh, how crazy to have fallen so quickly.

"Look at this place," I said, gesturing at the lively scene before us. "It's like something straight out of a storybook. There's an enchanting energy about it, don't you think?"

Elijah nodded, his eyes reflecting the wonder of the moment. "Absolutely. I've always loved this time of year. There's a sense of mystery in the air, as if anything could happen."

"Exactly," I agreed, feeling the excitement bubble up within me. As we continued to stroll through the market, I paused to soak in every detail of the evening: the flickering shadows cast by jack-o'-lanterns, the chorus of laughter and chatter that filled the night, the warmth radiating from our clasped hands. It all felt like a dream, one I never wanted to wake up from.

"Ronan," Elijah murmured, bringing me back to reality. "I'm so glad we're experiencing this together. It feels... special."

"Me too," I admitted, my heart swelling with affection for the man beside me.

The soft glow of the pumpkin lanterns cast an intimate light over Elijah and me as we wandered further into the bustling Halloween market.

"Hey, Ronan," Elijah whispered, leaning closer. "I really appreciate you opening up to me earlier. I can't even begin to imagine how difficult it must have been to be so vulnerable."

"Thanks, Elijah," I replied, my voice hushed as well. "It's...challenging but knowing I'm safe with you makes it a bit easier." I glanced at him, noticing the way the flickering light danced across his hair and illuminated the sincerity in his eyes.

"Same here," he agreed softly. "Sharing my past experiences with you is something I never thought I'd be able to do. And yet, here we are."

Our conversation flowed effortlessly, each topic bouncing to the next. The tension between us grew, both electrifying and tender – a delicate dance of emotions that drew us closer together.

"I've been afraid," I admitted. "Afraid of what others would think, of not being enough, of never finding someone who truly understands me."

Elijah squeezed my hand gently. "We all have our fears, Ronan. But it's moments like these, when we share our deepest insecurities, that we realize we're not alone."

"Exactly," I said, feeling a jolt spread through me at the realization that we were building something special, something real. "I never thought I'd find someone who could see past my quirks and awkwardness, but here you are."

"Here I am," Elijah confirmed, a smile tugging at the corner of his lips. "And I'm not going anywhere."

A gentle breeze rustled the autumn leaves as we stood there, side by side, our hands still clasped together. The sound of laughter and joy from the other marketgoers seemed to fade away, leaving just the two of us in this intimate moment. Our eyes locked, Elijah's warm brown gaze held a depth that both comforted and stirred something within me.

"Ronan," he whispered, his voice trembling with emotion. "I've never felt like this before."

"Neither have I." As the words left my lips, I knew it was true – the connection between us had grown stronger than anything I'd ever experienced before. It was both exhilarating and terrifying, but above all else, it was precious.

Our noses brushed slightly, and we both exhaled softly, our breaths mingling in the cool night air. Anticipation thrummed through my veins; a tingling sensation that made time seem to slow down as if suspended by some unseen force. The longing to close the distance between us grew, and I could see the same desire mirrored in Elijah's eyes.

"Can I...?" he trailed off, not needing to finish the question. My nod was almost imperceptible, but he understood. We were on the cusp of something magical, something that would bind us closer than ever before.

"Ronan," he whispered once more. "I'm scared."

"Me too," I confessed. "But we're learning together, right?"

"Right," he agreed, his smile returning, albeit tentatively. "Together."

As our faces inched closer, the world around us seemed to fade away entirely, eclipsed by the weight of this shared moment. The anticipation was an electric current, coursing through us both, connecting us on a level neither of us had ever known before.

As the final centimeters disappeared between us, my senses sharpened to a razor's edge. The warmth of Elijah's breath against my lips sent shivers cascading down my spine. Our eyes flickered shut simultaneously, as if guided by some unseen maestro.

"Ronan," he whispered once more, the sound both a prayer and a promise.

"Yes."

And then our lips met.

Softly, tentatively, we explored each other's mouths, the gentle pressure sending shockwaves of pure emotion coursing through me. I felt the contours of his lips – full and inviting – molding perfectly against my own. Our connection deepened, an addiction I never knew existed.

The kiss seemed to exist outside the boundaries of time, a moment suspended with only the two of us tethered together in an intimate embrace. My hand found its way to the small of his back, pulling him closer as if trying to meld our bodies, our souls, into one.

I'd never known such tenderness before, such delicate vulnerability shared between two people. Our pasts, our fears, and all of our hopes hung in the balance, buoyed by this singular act of trust. It was a powerful emotional stir, one that threatened to sweep us away on a tide of unspoken words and quivering heartbeats.

Slowly, reluctantly, we broke apart, our foreheads coming to rest against each other as we caught our breath. His smile was shy but radiant, a reflection of the emotions swirling within us both. We didn't need words – not now, not when our hearts spoke volumes.

"Thank you," he murmured. "For being here, for trusting me."

"Thank you," I echoed. "For showing me that love can be this beautiful."

As we stood there, hand in hand beneath the twinkling lights and pumpkin lanterns, I knew that we had forged something unbreakable. Our future together was still uncertain, still a book yet to be completed, but the love we shared was real and true.

"Ronan, together?"

"Of course," I repeated, sealing the promise with another tender kiss. Together, we would face whatever challenges life had in store for us, buoyed by the love that had taken root within our hearts. And as the magic of the Halloween season swirled around us, I knew that our sweet beginning was just the first step on a journey we were destined to walk hand in hand.

He blushed at my brazenness, but I could see the pride shining in his eyes. "I guess we've both come a long way, huh?"

"Definitely," I agreed, feeling my own face heat up. "But we'll keep going."

3: Ronan

"Hey, Ronan!" Harper's voice rang out like a chime, laced with warmth and familiarity. Her short blonde hair framed her face in its usual pixie cut, the sun highlighting its golden hues.

"Hi, Harper," I replied as my gaze darted to meet hers before returning to the floor. The thought of the conversation we were about to have gnawed at the pit of my stomach.

"Alright, big brother, what's up? You sounded pretty serious on the phone." She settled onto a stool by the counter, her blue eyes searching my face with concern.

Taking a deep breath, I began, "I... I've been struggling lately. With commitment... and being vulnerable, emotionally. With Elijah." I forced the words out, feeling the weight of them hang in the air.

"Ronan, I'm worried about you." Harper's voice softened, her brow furrowing as she regarded me. "You know I love you, right? And that I want what's best for you?"

"Of course," I murmured, my chest tightening at her sincerity.

"Then you know I have to ask: are you sure about Elijah?" Her question hung heavy between us. "His intentions... I just want to be sure he's not taking advantage of you."

"Harper, he's... he's not like that," I insisted, my voice wavering slightly as I clenched my fists, the anxiety bubbling within me. "He's kind and caring, and I believe he loves me."

"Ronan," she sighed, her gaze never leaving mine. "I'm not trying to be difficult. I just need you to be cautious. Your heart is so big, and I don't want it to get broken. Promise me you'll be careful?"

"I promise, Harper," I whispered, my heart aching as I saw the love and concern etched across her face. "Thank you for being here for me."

"Always, Ronan." She smiled gently, reaching out to squeeze my hand. "You're my big brother, and I love you. That means I'll always have your back, no matter what."

As we sat there, bathed in the golden sunlight streaming from the window, I felt the weight of Harper's love and support buoying me. I'd been feeling more and more insecure lately. About his prior relationships with women. I didn't know how to process it.

Harper sighed, "when are you going to introduce us? I'm starting to feel like there's something wrong with him because you keep ducking me when I ask to meet him."

"Harper, I promise you, Elijah's love is genuine," I said, my voice soft but determined. "He's been so patient with me, even when I struggle to express myself."

"Ronan, I want to believe that, but I can't help worrying about you," Harper replied

"Look, I know I don't have much experience in dating," I admitted, feeling a knot of anxiety in my stomach. "But I've seen how Elijah is with me, and with others. He's warm, kind, and understanding. The way he looks at me... it's like he sees something worth loving, even if I can't always see it myself."

"Wow, Ronan," she paused, visibly moved by my words. "I never thought I'd hear you talk about someone like that."

"Neither did I, but here we are." I chuckled nervously, rubbing the back of my neck. "I'm just as surprised as you are."

"Okay, I'll trust your judgment for now." Harper sighed, giving me a small, tentative smile. "But I'm still going to keep an eye on him."

"Thank you, Harper," I whispered, relief flooding through me. "That means a lot to me."

As we sat there, she seemed to study me intently, her brows furrowed in concentration. I shifted uncomfortably under her gaze, worried about what she might be thinking.

"Ronan, do you think your autism plays a part in your struggles with emotional vulnerability?"

"Probably," I confessed after a pause. "It's hard for me to understand and express my feelings sometimes. But I'm trying."

"Hey, I'm proud of you, Ronan," she smiled warmly, reaching out to squeeze my hand again. "And I'm sure Elijah can see how hard you're working at it. You're perfect the way you are."

"Thanks, Harper." I returned her smile, grateful for her understanding and support.

"Ronan, I'm going to spend some time with Elijah," Harper announced one sunny afternoon as we sat in the cozy kitchen of my apartment. "I want to get to know him better and understand his intentions towards you."

"Really?" I asked, taken aback by her decision. I knew she wanted to meet him, but this was sprung on me too suddenly. My nerves sent my heartrate sky rocketing. "I mean... sure, if you think that will help."

"Good," she replied with determination. "I'll be watching him closely. He better be prepared for 21 questions."

Over the next few weeks, Harper made an effort to be around Elijah and me more often. She accompanied us on walks through the park and joined us for movie nights at home. I couldn't help but feel a little anxious, knowing how protective Harper was of me.

One evening, after a particularly challenging day at school, I had come home to create. I found myself struggling to hold back tears. My hands shook as I attempted to mold the delicate sugar flowers, each petal crumbling under my touch.

"Hey, Ronan," Elijah's comforting voice broke through my frustration, his warm hand resting gently on my shoulder. "Take a deep breath. We can do this together."

"Thanks," I murmured, leaning into his touch as he held my hands, helping me craft the intricate blooms.

"See? You're doing great," he encouraged, his infectious smile lighting up his face.

"Wow, you two make quite the team," Harper chimed in from the doorway, her arms crossed as she observed us. I could see the beginnings of a genuine smile tugging at the corners of her mouth.

"Thanks, Harper," Elijah grinned, his eyes never leaving mine. "We're lucky to have each other."

As the days went by, I noticed a subtle shift in Harper's demeanor. The skepticism that had once clouded her eyes seemed to dissipate, replaced by something warmer and more accepting.

One night, as the three of us sat on the couch watching a romantic comedy, I couldn't help but sneak a glance at Harper. She was laughing along with Elijah, their heads close together as they shared a bowl of popcorn.

"Ronan," she whispered to me during a quiet moment in the movie, her eyes shining with sincerity. "I want you to know that I see how much Elijah cares for you. He's been patient and supportive, and that means a lot."

"Thank you, Harper," I replied. "That means the world to me."

"I'll be here for you, Ronan," she promised. "No matter what."

In that moment, surrounded by the warmth of my sister's understanding and my unwavering love of Elijah, I finally began to believe that maybe – just maybe – we could make this work.

A gentle breeze rustled the leaves of the old oak tree in our shared back courtyard, casting dappled shadows on the soft grass beneath my feet. I watched as Elijah and Harper sat together on a cozy blanket, their laughter filling the air with a joyful melody. The late afternoon sun showered everything in a warm glow, making the scene before me feel like a dream.

"Ronan, come join us!" Elijah called, waving his hand enthusiastically. As I approached them, Harper shifted to make room for me on the blanket, her eyes shining with warmth.

"Let's talk about Ronan," she said, turning to Elijah with a soft smile. "He's so talented with his candy creations, don't you think?"

"Absolutely," Elijah agreed, nodding earnestly. "And not just that, he's also incredibly kind and thoughtful. It amazes me every day."

I felt my cheeks heat up at their compliments; accepting compliments had never been my strong suit. They continued to exchange stories of times when I had made them proud or happy, and it warmed my heart to see how much they both cared about me.

"Harper, I promise you, I love your brother more than anything in this world," Elijah confessed, his voice sincere and steady. "I'll do whatever it takes to make him happy and ensure he feels safe and loved."

"I believe you," Harper replied softly.

As their conversation deepened, Elijah opened up to Harper about his struggles with bisexuality, explaining how societal expectations had often left him feeling judged and misunderstood.

"It's been difficult, you know?" he admitted, his voice cracking slightly. "But being with Ronan has helped me accept myself more, and I hope I've done the same for him."

Listening to Elijah's words, I was struck by the vulnerability and honesty he displayed. This was a side of him I had seen before, but it was touching to witness the depth of his trust in Harper.

"Thank you for sharing that with me, Elijah," Harper said, her voice gentle. "I can understand how hard it must have been for both of you. But seeing how much you care for Ronan, and how dedicated you are to making him happy, makes all the difference."

Elijah smiled at her. "I'm glad we've had this chance to talk, Harper. It means a lot to me to know that you're on our side."

"Of course," she assured him, her expression softening even more. "I'll always be here for my brother, and now, for you too."

As their conversation continued, I felt a profound sense of relief and happiness wash over me. The bond forming between Elijah and Harper was comforting. My family hadn't been the most accepting of my celibacy. My mom tried hooking me up with every church lady's daughter she could find, which always led to disaster. Eventually, I just stopped trying to meet people.

"I need to head home, Ronan, I have a meeting tomorrow. I'll call you after, okay?" Elijah said, giving me a quick peck before getting up.

"Okay, I'll chat to you then!" I stood and made my way home to the apartment, Harper in tow.

I sat on the porch swing, lost in thought. The sun was melting into the horizon, splashing vibrant hues of orange and pink across the sky. I smiled at the sight, reminded of the colorful candies I loved to create.

"Hey, Ronan," Harper's voice broke through my reverie, her presence a welcome comfort. She took a seat beside me on the swing, gently nudging my shoulder. "I've got something I want to talk to you about."

"Of course, what's up?" I asked, my curiosity piqued.

Harper hesitated for a moment, her eyes searching mine before she spoke. "All this time I've been spending with Elijah getting to know him better, I have to admit... I was wrong about him."

"I'm glad to hear it." I smiled. I'd known her mind had been changing, but hearing her admit it was sweet. "What changed your mind?"

"Seeing how he is with you, Ronan," she explained, her tone sincere. "The way he looks at you, the compassion and understanding he shows... it's clear that he loves you deeply."

"Thank you, Harper," I murmured. "Your support means more to me than you could ever know."

"Of course, Ronan," she replied, reaching over to squeeze my hand. "I just want you to be happy. And if Elijah makes you happy, then I'm all for it."

"Trust me, he does," I assured her. "He's been such a positive influence in my life. I don't know what I would do without him."

"Then I'm glad you found each other," she said, her smile radiant.

We sat there on the porch swing, watching the sun dip below the horizon. Her words had lifted a weight off my shoulders, allowing me to fully embrace the love and happiness that Elijah brought into my life.

"Harper?" I asked hesitantly, fidgeting with the hem of my shirt. "Do you think...I mean, am I enough for him?"

"Ronan," she replied, meeting my gaze with a fierce determination. "You are more than enough. You're kind, talented, and have the biggest heart of anyone I know. Don't ever doubt your worth."

"Thank you," I whispered, feeling tears prick at the corners of my eyes. Harper's support was a balm to my soul, she had always soothed my brains negative thoughts.

"Anytime, big brother," she said softly, leaning against me as we continued to watch the sunset.

The gentle sway of the porch swing and the soft rustle of leaves overhead provided a comforting backdrop as Harper and I sat, side by side.

"Harper, thank you," I began hesitantly, twisting my fingers around each other. "Your acceptance means everything to me. I've looked up to you since we were little, and your approval... well, it's vital."

She turned her head, eyes filled with understanding. "Ronan, I'm sorry I ever doubted Elijah. You deserve happiness, and it never mattered to me who it was with, just that you were treated right."

"I know things haven't been easy for either of us, but we've grown so much together. I'm grateful for that."

"Me too, Ronan." Harper's voice softened, a smile curving her lips. "We're stronger now because of it."

"Definitely," I agreed. We shared a moment of comfortable silence, just taking in the beauty of the evening.

"Hey," Harper suddenly said, nudging me gently with her elbow. "You remember how we used to make up stories about the people who lived in our neighborhood when we were kids?"

I let out a chuckle, recalling our wild childhood imaginations. "Oh, yeah! Like Mr. Thompson being a secret superhero or Mrs. Jenkins being a time-traveling historian."

"Exactly!" She laughed, her eyes glinting with mischief. "What do you think our story would be if someone made one up about us?"

"Umm," I pondered, an idea forming in my mind. "We'd be sibling inventors who create magical concoctions that can cure any ailment and bring happiness to all who taste them."

"Ooh, I like that," Harper grinned. "And we'd have a secret lab hidden beneath the shop and we can douse grumpy people with them."

"Love that." I said, feeling my spirits lift as we delved further into our fantastical tale.

As the sun dipped below the horizon, I realized that it didn't matter what imaginary stories others might weave about us. What mattered was the love and understanding between Harper and me. Our bond had been tested in the past, but it also had grown stronger with each new situation we faced together.

The scent of cocoa and sugar filled the air as I prepared the shop to open. Ms. Wells hated when the shop was opened a minute past 8. As I glanced out the window, I noticed Elijah approaching the door.

"Hey, Ronan," he greeted me with that contagious smile of his, making my heart flutter. "How's your day going?"

"Good," I replied with a smile. "I just finished making these truffles."

"Those look delicious," he said, leaning over the counter for a closer look. "Would you mind if I sample one?"

"Of course not," I chuckled, handing him a small piece. His eyes lit up as he savored the rich chocolate, and my chest swelled with pride.

"Ronan, these are amazing!" he exclaimed, his enthusiasm warming me to my core.

"Thank you," I murmured. Just as I was about to lean over for a kiss, none other than my sister burst in the door.

"I'm just stalking Elijah, no big deal. Oh, truffles, don't mind if I do!" She said, making herself completely at home. "Anyway, the real reason I wanted to meet you both, is that mom and dad want to meet Elijah. They're... being a bit difficult. But I've got your backs."

"Thank you, Harper," Elijah replied. "I don't want to make any enemies."

"Good," Harper nodded, giving us a determined look. "Now, if anyone so much as breathes a word against you two, they'll have to answer to me."

"Harper, you don't need to –" I began, but she cut me off with a wave of her hand.

"Ronan, I know I was skeptical at first, but I can see how much you care for each other," she said earnestly. "You deserve to be happy, both of you. And I'll do whatever it takes to make sure that happens."

"Thank you, sis," I whispered.

"Besides," she added with a playful smirk, "I'm pretty sure Elijah's candy addiction is keeping this place in business. Or maybe it's his addiction to you. It's certainly not because Mrs. Wells knows how to make anything that tastes remotely half-decent."

"Hey!" Elijah protested, feigning offense. "I just appreciate the finer things in life, like Ronan's candies."

"Whatever you say," Harper teased, rolling her eyes affectionately.

4: Elijah

The bell above the door jingled as we stepped into our favorite café, and I couldn't suppress a grin. As Ronan and I made our way to a cozy corner table, the familiar scent of fresh-baked pastries and coffee filled my nostrils. Our usual spot welcomed us like an old friend, the warm wooden tones of the furniture creating an intimate atmosphere.

"Two hot chocolates, please," I said to the friendly barista behind the counter. She nodded and quickly got to work on our order. While we waited, Ronan's fingers drummed lightly against the table, his hair falling across his forehead in a way that made my heart leap.

"Thanks for coming with me today," I told him, leaning in closer. "I've had this idea bouncing around in my head for ages, and I just need to share it with someone."

"Of course, Elijah." Ronan said, watching me carefully. His shy smile emerged, warming my heart even more than our steaming cups of hot chocolate ever could. I took a sip, letting the rich, velvety liquid fill my senses, before diving into the exciting news.

"Okay, so you know how much we love candy, right?" I began, my eyes sparkling with enthusiasm. Ronan chuckled and nodded, well aware of my sweet tooth. "Well, I've been thinking about it a lot lately, and I want us to open a candy store!"

His eyebrows shot up in surprise, but a glimmer of interest flickered in his eyes. "Really? That sounds amazing, Elijah! Tell me more."

"Think about it, Ronan," I continued. "A place where people can come together and enjoy the magic of candy – where we can bring happiness to others through our shared passion for sweets."

As I spoke, Ronan's eyes softened, the corners of his mouth turning up in a smile that reached all the way to his soul. It was moments like these – when our dreams and desires meshed seamlessly – that reminded me how truly special our connection was.

"Wow, Elijah," he breathed, his fingers intertwining with mine on the table. "This... this is amazing."

"You'll be in charge of everything creative. I'll be the taste tester, of course. But you will have free creative license, down to the name."

Ronan's smile grew wider, his eyes sparkling with possibility. "Elijah, that sounds absolutely amazing. We could craft candies based on flavors that evoke memories and emotions." The thought of working together to build something so magical left an undeniable warmth in my chest.

"Exactly!" I exclaimed. "And the decor – oh, it has to be whimsical and inviting. A place where people feel like they've stepped into a fairy tale."

"Maybe we could have a huge tree with branches reaching out across the ceiling, twinkling with fairy lights," Ronan suggested.

"Perfect! And the walls could be adorned with murals of enchanted forests and mythical creatures," I added, lost in the vision of our store. "What do you think about having little nooks and crannies filled with plush, cozy seating, where customers can relax while enjoying their treats?"

Ronan's eyes lit up at the idea. "That sounds wonderful, babe. A peaceful sanctuary where people can escape from the hustle and bustle of everyday life."

We sat there, dreaming up more ideas for our candy store, each suggestion sparking another, building upon the last. It felt like we were painting a beautiful picture together, stroke by stroke, until a masterpiece emerged before our very eyes.

"Ronan, I can't believe how perfectly our dreams align," I murmured. "I feel like we can really make this happen."

"Me too, Elijah," he agreed. "I've never felt so sure about anything in my life."

"Hey, I've got an idea for the name of our candy store," I said, the words tumbling out of my mouth before I could even think them through.

Ronan looked at me, his eyes wide and eager. "Yeah? What is it?"

"Twisted Candy Canes!" I exclaimed, grinning as I thought about Ronan's love for the holiday treat. "I know how much you adore candy canes, and it'll be a unique spin on something classic."

His face instantly lit up, and his excitement was infectious. "Elijah, I love it! It's so... us." He paused, his smile becoming more determined. "We've got this. We can make Twisted Candy Canes the best candy store in town."

"Absolutely," I agreed. As we brainstormed ideas for our store, I allowed myself to get swept into thoughts of the future. One where we existed together, making our dreams come true.

"Imagine the look on people's faces when they step into our store," Ronan mused, his eyes sparkling with anticipation. "We'll create a world of pure imagination, where everyone can escape their worries and indulge in something sweet."

"Exactly," I nodded. "And we won't stop there. We'll be experimenting with new flavors and concoctions, pushing the boundaries of what people expect from a candy store."

"Like our very own Willy Wonka," Ronan chuckled, his enthusiasm contagious. "I can't wait to get started, Elijah. This journey will be amazing, I just know it."

"Me too, Ronan. I've never felt so certain about anything in my life." *Except you.*

As we sat there, our fingers entwined and our hearts full of excitement, I knew that we were on the cusp of something extraordinary. Twisted Candy Canes was just the beginning – our sweet love story was only getting started.

"Alright, so we have the name and the vision for our store," I began, feeling more excited with each passing moment. "Now, we should brainstorm ideas for our signature candy apple – something that truly represents us and our journey together."

"Great idea, Elijah," Ronan agreed. "Let's think about what makes our love special and unique."

"Definitely," I nodded, my mind racing with ideas. "Well, one of the first things that comes to mind is how we met at the Halloween fair... maybe caramel?"

"True," Ronan said thoughtfully, his fingers tapping on the table as he considered the possibilities. "I like the idea of using apples as a base. And since you're all about adventure and trying new things, maybe we can play with some unexpected flavors?"

"Absolutely!" I exclaimed, loving the direction this conversation was taking. "Do you remember that time you made those ones with chili flakes? That unexpected kick really took them to another level."

Ronan's face lit up at the memory, and he quickly pulled out a small notebook from his bag. "Yes! That was such a fun day. We could definitely draw inspiration from that experience." He started jotting down flavor combinations, his pen moving rapidly across the page.

As I watched Ronan scribble away, I watched in fascination. His mind was truly unique. I could never come up with idea's as fast as he could. He was something else.

"Okay, I think I've got it," Ronan announced, looking up at me with a mix of excitement and anticipation. "What if our signature candy apple combines the sweetness of caramel, the tanginess of green apples, and a hint of spice from chili flakes, topped with a dash of cinnamon and a sprinkle of nutmeg?"

"Wow, that sounds amazing, Ronan!" I enthused. "I think it perfectly captures the essence of our love – sweet and comforting, with just enough excitement to keep things interesting."

"Exactly," Ronan agreed, his shy smile growing wider as he continued to scribble in his notebook. "We could even add a touch of gold leaf to make it truly special, like a little bit of magic that represents the enchantment we bring to each other's lives."

"Ronan, that's beautiful," I said softly, moved by his words. "I can't wait to share this amazing journey with you, creating a world of sweetness and love for everyone who steps through the doors of Twisted Candy Canes."

The moment Ronan's pen touched the notebook once more, I couldn't tear my gaze away. His focused expression and the way his hand moved gracefully across the page left me in awe. It was as if he'd found the perfect balance of strength and delicacy, much like our love story. The little crease between his eyes as he concentrated was endearing and I yearned to lean over and kiss it.

"Hey, Elijah," Ronan said suddenly, glancing up at me with those deep, thoughtful eyes. "I think I've got something you'll want to hear."

"Really? What do you have in mind?"

"Okay, so," he began, excitement dancing in his voice. "For a pie dish, I'm thinking we combine cinnamon and brown sugar for warmth, McIntosh apples, then add a splash of orange zest to give it some brightness. And finally, a coating of dark chocolate for that touch of mystery and depth, just like us."

"Ronan, that sounds incredible!" I gushed. "But how did you come up with such a fantastic idea?"

He grinned sheepishly. "Well, I was thinking about our first real date, when we took that long walk through the park at dusk. Remember how the air smelled of cinnamon from the nearby bakery, and the way the setting sun cast an orange glow on everything? And then there was that moment when our hands accidentally brushed against each other, sending shivers down my spine...it felt like pure magic."

"Wow," I breathed out, feeling the goosebumps rise on my skin as I recalled that unforgettable night. "You've really captured the essence of our love in this recipe, haven't you?"

Ronan's face flushed with pride, and he nodded. "That's what I was hoping for. I want to create something that would remind us of our journey together. An ode to us."

"Ronan," I whispered. "You never cease to amaze me. Your dedication, creativity, and your beautiful heart...they make me fall for you even more every day."

"Thank you, Elijah. I feel the same way about you. And I can't wait to embark on this incredible adventure with you, hand in hand."

"Neither can I," I agreed, our gazes locked as we shared a moment of perfect understanding. Leaning forward, I brushed my lips against his, holding him tightly before slowly letting go. This man breathes life into me.

The waitress kept giving us dirty looks. I suppose we'd exhausted our time here, but I didn't want to leave. It was peaceful here.

The warmth of Ronan's hand in mine was like sunshine, bright and full of life. Our fingers intertwined naturally, as if they were meant to fit together this way. In the quiet of the cozy café, I found myself lost in his eyes, swimming in their depths.

"Ronan," I whispered. His gaze met mine, and for a moment, we existed in a world that belonged only to us.

"Wait," he said hesitantly, his dark eyes searching mine for answers I didn't even know the question to yet. "I don't understand, and it's been bothering me. If you've only ever dated women before, why are you with me now? What makes this different?"

My breath caught in my throat as I mulled over his question, struggling to find the right words. The cozy atmosphere of the café seemed to shrink around us, making the air feel thick and heavy. I glanced down at our entwined hands, the sight grounding me as I delved into my thoughts.

"What made you suddenly think of this?"

"I just... it's been on my mind for a while and I haven't really known how to express it, and with us moving into business ownership and making this huge decision, I need to know. I need to understand you. I need my mind to quiet against the raging thoughts of not being good enough. Just answer me, please."

"Ronan," I began softly, lifting my gaze to meet his once more. "The truth is, I never really thought about gender when it came to love. It wasn't about whether someone was a man or a woman; it was about the connection we shared."

"Then...why have you only been with women?" Ronan asked, his voice wavering.

"Maybe it was just chance," I admitted, my heart aching at the vulnerability I saw in his eyes. "Or maybe it took meeting you for me to fully understand that part of myself." A tender smile played on my lips as I added, "You're the one who makes me feel like I can truly be myself, without any reservations or expectations."

"Really?" His voice trembled with emotion, and I could see the hope flickering in his eyes.

"Absolutely," I assured him, squeezing his hand for emphasis. "Being with you has opened up a whole new world for me, Ronan. One where love knows no boundaries, and every moment spent together is a gift."

A slow, hesitant smile spread across his face, and I could see the relief washing over him. But there was still a glimmer of doubt in his eyes, a lingering question that threatened to overshadow our happiness.

"Are you sure?" he asked. "Are you really sure about us?"

"More sure than I've ever been about anything," I replied without hesitation, my heart swelling with love for the man sitting across from me.

"Even if it's something new and... unexpected?" Ronan questioned, biting his lip nervously.

"Especially then," I whispered, leaning in closer. "You're the one that sets my heart on fire, and the one who makes me excited to get up in the morning."

"Wow, that's beautiful," Ronan murmured. "I suppose I've always known I was attracted to both men and women; it's just been a part of who I am. I've just never found one I wanted to be with. Until I met you.

"In the end, what matters most is that we found each other. Love isn't a destination, but a journey that brings us closer to understanding ourselves and the world around us."

"True," Ronan agreed, his eyes never leaving mine as his thumb gently stroked the back of my hand. "I'm grateful for this journey with you, Elijah."

"Me too," I said.

5: Elijah

I t was one of those endless sunny fall days; the sun hung stubbornly in the sky as if it too refused to leave the golden paradise. The smell of sugar and cocoa filled the air. I leaned against the counter, my eyes fixed on Ronan, who was delicately pouring melted chocolate into a mold.

"Hey," I said softly, trying to catch his eye. "How's it going?"

"Good," he replied, his voice barely more than a whisper. His hands shook ever so slightly, betraying his uncertainty. I could see the nervousness in his movements, the way he hesitated before each step.

I bit my lip, feeling the weight of my own insecurities bearing down on me. My past relationships with women had been a roller-coaster of emotions, leaving me both thrilled and devastated. It wasn't that I didn't love them – I did, passionately – but something inside me whispered that there was more to my heart's desire.

"Ronan," I began hesitantly, my heart racing. "I wanted to talk to you about... well, about us."

"Sure," he said, pausing his work and giving me his full attention. "What's up?"

I sighed, struggling to find the right words. "I... I just want to make sure I'm doing everything I can for you, you know? I don't want you to feel like I don't understand your needs or anything like that."

Ronan's eyes softened as he came around the counter to sit beside me. "Elijah, you're doing great. Why are you worried about this?"

"Because..." I paused, taking a deep breath before continuing. "I've been thinking a lot about my past relationships after our discussion. How they didn't work out. I feel guilty about some of the things I did, or didn't do, and I don't want to repeat those mistakes with you."

"Thank you for being honest with me," Ronan said gently, placing a hand on mine. "I appreciate that. But you should know that I have my own insecurities too. We're both still learning and growing."

"That's true," I admitted. "I guess I'm just scared that I won't be enough for you, or that I won't be able to be the partner you need."

"Hey. We can only do our best, right? And we'll learn from each other along the way. As long as we keep talking and communicating openly, I think we'll figure it out."

"Thank you, Ronan," I murmured, feeling some of the weight lift from my shoulders. "I want you to know that I'm here for you too. If there's anything you need or want to talk about, don't hesitate to bring it up. We're a team, right?"

"Right," he agreed. "A team."

As the evening light streamed through the window, bathing the room in a warm golden hue, I watched Ronan's lean fingers work their magic on the delicate pieces of candy he was crafting. The sight of him so absorbed in his passion filled my heart with love and awe.

"Ronan," I began. "There's something I need to share with you."

He paused, turning those soulful eyes toward me, his hair falling softly across his forehead. "What is it, Elijah?" he asked gently, concern etched into his handsome features.

"Throughout my life, I've been drawn to people who needed me - people I could fix or support in some way," I confessed, my chest tightening with the weight of my past. "But I don't want to fix you, I want you to feel free to be who you are. Do I ever make you feel like you have to be someone else?"

Ronan's gaze softened, and he reached out to take my hand. "Elijah, you've never made me feel that way. I have my own insecurities, as we discussed earlier. I don't think either of us should be this concerned, but it just goes to show how deeply we care about each other."

The honesty in his voice resonated deep within me, and I squeezed his hand in reassurance. "We really do, don't we?"

"I love you from the core to the ozone and beyond the Milky Way."

"I love you too, babe," I said, chuckling in spite of myself.

"Maybe let's set some goals for ourselves, for our relationship. To help us grow and address our concerns. I feel like addressing everything all in one day is kind of overwhelming, so maybe we can figure out a better method."

I nodded, feeling a sense of excitement at the prospect of setting goals together. "How about we start by making time for regular check-ins? Just to make sure we're both on the same page and feeling heard."

"Sounds like a great idea," Ronan agreed. "And let's also work on understanding each other's insecurities, and maybe being able to throw in some unexpected love now and then. Maybe we can read up on emotional intelligence, or even attend a workshop or two together?"

"Absolutely," I said, already imagining us learning and growing together. "In fact, I recently came across a book that might be perfect for us – 'The Language of Emotions.' Let's read it together and discuss what we learn."

"Deal," Ronan agreed, smiling warmly at me. "And one last thing - let's not forget to have fun together. Life can be serious, but our love should be a source of joy and happiness."

"Couldn't agree more," I responded with a wide grin, feeling lighter than I had in days.

We lapsed into silence for a few moments. We had overcome minor bumps and bruises so far, but what concerned me was whether he would clam up if something major came up. Maybe it was time to be more aggressively passionate about him so that he knew without a doubt that I'd always stand by him.

"Ronan," I said softly, looking into his eyes, "I have never been more certain of anything in my life. Together, we can face any challenge that comes our way."

"Me too," he replied, the corner of his mouth turning upward in a tender smile. "Together, we're the candy apple clusters we made on that very first fated meeting."

I couldn't help but smile, feeling the pull of his presence drawing me in. Our faces were mere inches apart now, and my breath hitched at the sight of his slightly parted lips. It was in that instant I realized just how much our connection had deepened; not only through our conversations but also through the vulnerability we had shared.

Our lips met in a passionate kiss, sealing our commitment to one another. I felt the electricity between us intensify, as if we were two magnets drawn together by an irresistible force. His hands found their way to my waist, pulling me even closer, while mine tangled in his hair, desperate to feel every inch of him.

As our kiss deepened, I felt the last remnants of doubt and insecurity begin to fade away. In their place, I found a growing sense of relief and reassurance in our love for one another. This was where I belonged, wrapped in Ronan's arms, surrounded by the sweet scent of his cologne and the warmth of his body pressed against mine.

Finally, we broke apart, both of us gasping for air after the intensity of our embrace. Ronan's eyes were filled with a mixture of happiness and relief, mirroring my own emotions. We had taken a crucial step together, facing our issues head-on.

"Let's make a promise. One we can hold onto when trouble comes," I whispered, my forehead resting against his as we caught our breath. "Promise me that we'll make an effort to understand, to be compassionate, and to really listen. That we won't just give up when we could have held on."

"I promise," Ronan said.

6: Elijah

As Ronan and I sat down together on the plush sofa, I couldn't help but feel a mixture of excitement and anxiety. My parents and Harper were on their way over for dinner, and although my family had always been supportive of our relationship, I worried they wouldn't understand our business venture. We'd have to start with an emotional plea. My mom loved hearing the why behind the what.

"Ronan. My family... they support us, but I can't shake this feeling that they won't truly understand." I glanced around the room, taking in the years of memories displayed on the walls. "I know they love me, but I'm not sure how they'll react to us doing this."

Ronan's hand found mine, giving it a gentle squeeze. "Elijah, we've faced challenges before, and we can face this one too. Your parents have always been kind to me. We'll make them see how much we mean to each other and how much Twisted Candy Canes means to our future."

I smiled at him. But deep down, I knew it wasn't just about convincing my family; I needed to address their concerns head-on. It was up to me to show them that what Ronan and I shared was real and lasting.

"Thank you, Ronan," I replied. "I understand their concerns, and I want to address them honestly. We're not just two people who happen to like candy. We share a passion for bringing joy to others through our creations, and we've built a strong bond because of it. I'll do everything in my power to make things right with them."

The reassuring warmth of Ronan's hand in mine did little to quell the butterflies in my stomach as we waited for my parents and his sister to arrive. My fingers unconsciously traced the intricate patterns on the embroidered tablecloth, betraying my anxiety.

"Hey," Ronan murmured. "Remember what we talked about earlier? We can face this together." He smiled softly, his dark eyes radiating a quiet strength that never failed to amaze me.

"Right," I agreed, forcing a smile. "Together."

The sound of the doorbell cut through the air like a knife, and I stood up abruptly, nearly knocking over my chair. I smoothed out my shirt, took a deep breath, and opened the front door to reveal my parents standing on the doorstep.

"Mom, Dad, welcome," I greeted them with as much composure as I could muster.

"Hello, Elijah," my mother replied, her voice warm but guarded. She looked past me into the living room, her gaze landing on Ronan. "Ronan, it's lovely to see you again."

"Thank you, Margaret," he replied with a smile.

As they stepped inside and removed their coats, my father's eyes met mine, and I could see the uncertainty etched in his expression. But there was something else, too—a willingness to listen and understand. It was a glimmer of hope I clung to as we moved into the living room to begin our evening together.

Seated around the dining table, bathed in the warm glow of candlelight, I felt a knot tighten in my chest. This was it—the moment to lay our hearts bare.

"Mom, Dad," I began, my voice steady but strained. "I know you have concerns, and I understand why. But I want you to know how much Ronan means to me." I glanced at him, his shy smile offering quiet reassurance. "We've faced so many challenges together, and he's been my rock through it all."

Ronan nodded, taking my hand as he added, "Elijah has brought so much joy into my life. He's there for me, even when things get tough. We've grown together, and I'm committed to our future."

Tears pricked my eyes as I recalled a particularly trying time. "When I lost my job, I was a mess. I thought everything was falling apart. But Ronan was there, encouraging me, picking up the pieces." My voice cracked, raw emotion spilling forth. "He helped me find the strength to start again, to rebuild."

"Before I met Elijah, I struggled with social situations," Ronan admitted. "I never felt like I fit in. But he's been so patient, helping me navigate this complex world." His eyes met mine, gratitude shining within their depths. "He's made me feel understood and accepted, like I belong."

"I've never known anyone as dedicated and passionate as Ronan," I confessed. "His drive to create beautiful, delicious candy inspires me every day. He's taught me that it's not just about making something sweet; it's about bringing happiness to others."

"Every time I see the excitement on someone's face when they taste one of my creations, I think of Elijah," Ronan said softly. "He's shown me the beauty in those small moments of joy."

As we shared our stories and laid our hearts bare, the weight of uncertainty began to lift. The connection between us was undeniable, a testament to the love that had blossomed despite adversity.

"Mom, Dad," I implored them, hope flickering like the candles before us. "We are stronger together, and we're committed to making this work. I hope you can see that, too, and find it in your hearts to support and invest in us."

After a long pause, I could see the tension in their expressions gradually melting away. Margaret's eyes softened, filling with a warmth that I hadn't seen in a long time, while Richard's furrowed brow eased as he studied us intently.

"Your love for each other is evident," Mom finally admitted, her voice wavering with emotion. "It's rare to find such a connection, and we'd be lying if we said we couldn't see it."

"Thank you, Mom," I whispered, relief washing over me like a gentle wave.

"However," Dad interjected cautiously, "we still have concerns about your future together."

"Understandable," Ronan chimed in. "But we'll face those challenges as a team."

As we continued to open up to them, the front door creaked, and footsteps echoed through the hallway. Harper appeared in the doorway, her short hair ruffled from the wind outside. She crossed her arms, studying us with guarded skepticism.

"Harper," Ronan greeted her nervously. "I'm so glad you're here."

"Wouldn't miss it," she replied. "I wanna invest in you guys, too."

"Thank you, Harper," I said earnestly. "We want nothing more than to bring joy to each other's lives."

The atmosphere in the room shifted, becoming lighter and filled with hope. We laughed and reminisced about the moments that had led us here.

Mom and Dad exchanged glances, then turned to us with open hearts. "Ronan," Mom began, "we may not understand everything about you yet, but your passion is clear. With Elijah's insights and your creativity... we'd be happy to invest in Twisted Candy Canes and get this venture off the ground."

"Thank you," Ronan whispered, his eyes shining with gratitude.

"Welcome to the family, son," Dad added, extending a hand towards him.

As we came together in a group embrace, I felt a surge of happiness and warmth envelop us all. Harper even joined in before leaving to make some tea. Once we had all settled into our seats again, she wanted to have the floor.

"Growing up, Ronan never really fit in," Harper explained. "He was always more interested in creating candy than making friends. People didn't understand him, and he often felt isolated and alone."

Tears welled up in my eyes as I listened to her recounting Ronan's struggles.

"Since meeting you," Harper continued, "I've seen a change in him. He's become more confident, more willing to take risks. It's clear that you've had a positive influence on his life, and for that, I'm grateful."

Relief washed over me, as if an enormous weight had been lifted from my shoulders. I could see the sincerity in Harper's eyes, and I knew she meant every word she said.

"As a result of how you've made my brother come out of his shell, I'd like to invest as well." She finished, bracing herself for the hugs we immediately gave her.

The mood in the room shifted again, this time towards warmth and camaraderie. Ronan and I began to share some of the lighthearted moments we'd experienced together—our first disastrous attempt at making the new caramel apple recipe, the time we got lost in a corn maze only to find ourselves back where we'd started.

As laughter filled the room, I watched our families' faces light up with joy. It felt whole.

"Remember that time we tried to recreate the scene from Ghost while making candy?" Ronan said with a chuckle, his cheeks flushing with embarrassment, and everyone burst into laughter.

"Or when we accidentally used salt instead of sugar in our chocolate truffles," I added, cringing at the memory. "I thought Mrs. Well's face was going to get stuck that way!"

My mother eventually pulled Ronan aside, and I strained to listen to their conversation, being the nosy man I was.

"Ronan," my mother began, her voice soft and warm, "this may have come as a surprise to us, but it's clear to see how much you two care for each other." She reached out and gently placed her hand on his, squeezing it reassuringly. "I just want to reiterate how lucky we are to have another son. You are everything to our Elijah, and therefore, you are everything to us. We want nothing more than for you both to succeed, in life, in love and in business."

"Thank you, Margaret," I heard Ronan reply. "That is everything."

My father cleared his throat and added, obviously having been eavesdropping himself, "We've seen how much joy you bring into Elijah's life. We want you both to feel loved and supported.

"Thank you, Richard," Ronan murmured, visibly touched by their words.

Having heard my parents' acceptance of not only our business, but also a reaffirmation of our relationship, my heart swelled with love and gratitude. I turned to Ronan, smiling at him as I whispered, "See? I told you we could do this together."

He blinked away tears, returning my smile with one of his own, full of love and relief. "Yeah. We did."

Harper, who had been silently observing the scene unfold, suddenly stepped forward, her arms open wide. "Group hug?" she suggested, her voice cracking slightly.

"Definitely," I agreed, pulling Ronan closer as my parents joined in. The five of us wrapped our arms around one another, allowing the warmth of our newfound unity to envelop us.

As we stood there, embracing each other, the room seemed to glow with something that went beyond the cozy ambiance created by the mementos and family photos surrounding us. It was the light of love, understanding, and acceptance that now filled the space, promising better days ahead for all of us.

"Okay, okay," my father finally said, breaking the hug and chuckling. "Let's not get too carried away. We still have dinner to enjoy."

"Right!" Mom exclaimed, wiping a stray tear from her eye. "I brought your favorite, Elijah—lasagna."

"Of course you did," I said. "Thank you, Mom."

As we sat down to eat, the excitement of the candy store filtered into the conversation.

Harper leaned forward, her earlier skepticism replaced with genuine curiosity. She had been listening with rapt attention as we described our décor ideas. "That sounds like a wonderful idea. What kind of candies will you make?"

"Everything from homemade chocolates to hard candies and gummies," Ronan replied, his voice full of enthusiasm. "I want to experiment with unique flavors and textures, blending old-fashioned techniques with new ideas."

"Sounds amazing!" Harper exclaimed, her eyes lighting up. "But how are you going to manage the business side of things?" She glanced at me, her eyebrows raised inquisitively.

"Actually, that's where I come in," I explained proudly. "I'll be handling the marketing, customer service, and overall management of the store, while Ronan focuses on creating delicious confections."

"Have you thought about a location for your store yet?" Mom asked, her interest piqued.

"Ronan and I have been scouting potential locations in town. We want a place that's easily accessible and has plenty of foot traffic," I answered, feeling the excitement build as we spoke.

"Count me in for anything you need help with," Harper offered, "I'm good with numbers, so if you ever need help with accounting or anything like that, let me know."

"Thank you, Harper," Ronan said.

"Your mother and I are here to support you too," Dad chimed in. "Whatever you need, just ask."

"Thank you all so much," I said. "It means the world to us to have your support."

"Sounds like you've really thought this through," Harper remarked. "You know, I'd like to help out if I can. Maybe I could design your logo or something?"

"Really?" I asked, touched by her offer. "That would be amazing, Harper. Thank you."

"Anything for my brother and his... well, sweetheart," she said with a teasing grin, winking at Ronan, who blushed but smiled back warmly.

"Thank you all for being so supportive," I said, my voice cracking with emotion. "I didn't expect this coming into this evening.

"Family sticks together, Elijah," Dad replied with pride. "And that includes Ronan now too."

"Exactly," Mom agreed, reaching out to place her hand atop mine and giving it a gentle squeeze. "You're both family, and we'll be here if you need us."

As our conversation continued, Ronan and I shared a look of pure happiness, our hands intertwined beneath the table. We knew there would be challenges ahead, but knowing our families had our back meant we wouldn't struggle alone.

Together, we could make our sweetest dreams come true.

7: Ronan

O *ne Year Later*

The finishing touches were all that remained. As I stood back to admire the colorful displays of candies and treats, Elijah swept into the room like a whirlwind, his hair bouncing with every step. "Ronan," he called, grinning from ear to ear. "Twisted Candy Canes is almost ready for its grand opening!"

"Almost" was the operative word, but we couldn't help but feel the excitement bubbling up in our chests. With each candy jar we filled and each sign we hung, our dreams inched closer to reality.

"Here, put this one on the top shelf," Elijah said, handing me a jar filled with shimmering gummy stars. His contagious smile spread across my face as I carefully placed it in its designated spot. We worked together, side by side, arranging sweets in an array of vibrant colors that would make any child's eyes widen in awe.

"Can you believe we did this?" I asked, allowing myself a moment to take it all in. The air was thick with anticipation and the scent of freshly made sweets – a fragrance that had become like home. The store felt alive, like a living, breathing testament to our love and dedication.

Elijah paused, looking around at the product of our hard work. "No, I can hardly believe it," he admitted, his voice soft and filled with wonder. "But we did it, Ronan. Together."

"Indeed, we did," I agreed, my chest swelling with pride. Our journey had been filled with overcoming inner turmoil, but the challenges we'd faced only made this moment sweeter. It was a beautiful thing, knowing that our love had not only endured but thrived, blossoming into something greater than either of us could have imagined. It was a big deal for me, being able to stick through something when I got uncomfortable. All I had ever wanted to do was run away. But not this time. Not with Elijah. I've sat in my feelings and as uncomfortable as that feels... I felt myself growing into a better man.

As we continued to prepare for the grand opening, I felt a sense of peace and contentment wash over me. We had come so far, and now, as we stood on the cusp of a new beginning, I knew that everything would be okay. For once, I was certain of our future – the future of Twisted Candy Canes, and the love that had brought us to this very moment.

As the door of Twisted Candy Canes swung open, laughter filled the shop. Familiar faces filled the store, their eyes widening in delight at the vibrant displays of sweets that Elijah and I had meticulously arranged.

"Congratulations, you two!" My younger sister, Lily, beamed as she wrapped her arms around both of us. "This place is like stepping into a dream!"

"Thank you, Lily," I replied, my heart swelling with pride. "We're so glad you could make it."

"Wouldn't miss it for the world!" She grinned before releasing us from her embrace, making her way to the candy-coated cookies we'd set out for our guests.

Elijah's parents approached next, hand-in-hand, their smiles just as warm and contagious as their son's. "Ronan, dear, you've done a marvelous job here. The store looks stunning!"

"Thank you, Margaret," I said politely, my cheeks flushing with pleasure. "It wouldn't have been possible without your support."

"It was our pleasure to help. You two deserve all the happiness in the world."

The store buzzed with excitement as friends and family members perused the shelves, their eyes twinkling like the fairy lights that adorned the walls. The atmosphere vibrated with joy and celebration, as well as the faint notes of a lively melody playing in the background. It was as if we had captured the essence of every childhood memory of candy stores and distilled it into this single moment.

"Isn't this incredible, Ronan?" Elijah whispered in my ear, his breath tickling my neck. "All these people, here to celebrate our love and achievement."

I nodded, unable to find the words to express the gratitude that welled up within me. It was a surreal feeling, seeing the people who meant the most to us gathered in one place, their support tangible and unwavering.

"Hey, lovebirds!" A jovial voice called out, pulling our attention away from each other. Our best friend, Oliver, grinned at us with his arm around his girlfriend, Clara. "You two have really outdone yourselves! This place is amazing."

"Thanks, Ollie," Elijah said, clapping him on the back. "We couldn't have done it without you both."

"True," Oliver agreed, feigning modesty. "But let's not forget the real stars of the show – your candy creations!"

"Speaking of which," Clara chimed in, her eyes twinkling mischievously, "I think I need to sample some more of those chocolate truffles."

"Try the raspberry-filled ones," I suggested, knowing they were her favorite. "I made a special batch just for today."

"Ooh, you're the best, Ronan!" She squealed before flitting off towards the treat table.

As they sauntered off, we made our way to the front of the store.

"Everyone, could I have your attention, please?" Elijah called out, his voice effortlessly carrying across the room as he stood beside me. The lively chatter gradually subsided, and all eyes turned in our direction.

"First off," he began, "Ronan and I want to thank you all for being here today. Your love and support have been invaluable in helping us make Twisted Candy Canes a reality."

I nodded, feeling my face flush with pride as I looked out at the sea of familiar faces. "We've been on an incredible journey together," I added, my voice slightly shaky, "and we're so grateful to have had all of you by our side."

"From late nights perfecting recipes to early mornings painting these walls," Elijah continued, gesturing around the room, "every bit of hard work has led to this moment. And as we stand here today, we feel a sense of accomplishment and fulfillment."

His hand found mine, giving it a gentle squeeze. Our eyes met, and I was struck by the depth of emotion in his gaze - a mirror of my own feelings. We shared a warm, knowing smile that spoke volumes.

"Here's to new beginnings," Elijah said, raising a glass filled with sparkling apple cider. "And to the sweetest adventure of our lives!"

"Cheers!" the crowd echoed, their voices blending into a harmonious chorus that seemed to resonate throughout the entire store. Glasses clinked, laughter rang out, and the festive atmosphere deepened as everyone raised their drinks in celebration.

"Hey," Elijah whispered, leaning towards me. "Let's sneak away for a moment."

"Alright," I agreed. "I'd like that." Crowds could be hard for me. I'm so grateful he knew me well enough to offer me an out for a while.

We slipped through the crowd, our hands intertwined, until we reached the small storage room hidden at the back of the store. I closed the door behind us, sealing ourselves in a world far removed from the joyous chaos outside.

"Ronan," Elijah breathed, his voice soft with emotion. He took a step closer, closing the distance between us. His hand gently cradled my face, his thumb tracing the curve of my cheekbone.

"Thank you," he murmured, his eyes locked onto mine with an intensity that made my breath hitch. "For this, for everything. I couldn't have done it without you."

"Neither could I," I admitted. "I've learned so much from you, Elijah. Not just about making candy, but about life, about myself."

A smile tugged at the corners of his lips, his eyes shining with warmth and love. "We make a great team, don't we?"

"We do," I confirmed.

Slowly, he leaned in, his breath mingling with mine. Our lips met in a tender kiss, a perfect fusion of sweetness and passion.

As we pulled apart, I rested my forehead against his, our breaths comingling in the small space between us. In that moment, I knew that no matter what challenges we might face in the future, we would face them together, hand in hand.

"Here's to us," I whispered, my voice full of love and certainty.

"Here's to us," Elijah echoed, his eyes reflecting the same conviction that swelled within my chest.

And as we stepped back into the celebration, our hearts beating in unison, I knew that this was just the beginning of a sweet adventure that would last a lifetime.

About the Author

Always being told she is a daydreamer, Stephanie uses her gifts for escaping into a fantasy world to bring those worlds to life. Unable to write solely in one genre, she has found herself enjoying writing a wide array of books. From historical fiction to fantasy, Stephanie loves it all. Hoping to instill a love of books in her children, Stephanie spends her days reading, writing and going on adventures with her family, allowing imagination to lead the way and creativity to write the stories. Her favorite adventures are the ones where her son leads them through magical portals to new lands in discovery of the mystery that lies there.

Contact Stephanie

You can contact Stephanie at: stephanieswann.author@gmail.com if you'd like to know more about her upcoming works!

Instagram: authorstephanieswann

https://www.instagram.com/authorstephanieswann/
Facebook: Stephanie Swann

https://www.facebook.com/StephanieSwannAuthor/
Tiktok: stephanieswannauthor

https://www.tiktok.com/@stephanieswannauthor
Other Links:

https://linktr.ee/stephanieswannauthor

Also By

Historical Fiction:

The Milkmaid: https://books2read.com/u/3yQJOe

The Betrayal: https://books2read.com/u/4NeqNx

Sweet Romance:

Twisted Candy Canes: https://books2read.com/u/bQeQqD

Fantasy Shifters:

Bonded to the Alpha Trio: https://books2read.com/u/mKVe95

Poetry:

Tempest. Vol 1: https://a.co/d/dUbYLA9

Tornado. Vol 2: https://a.co/d/gN5TcBp

Anthology:

Surviving The Unthinkable: https://a.co/d/cC5Ii45

Ream:

https://reamstories.com/stephanieswann

Printed in the USA
CPSIA information can be obtained
at www.ICGtesting.com
LVHW040717200824
788752LV00020B/247

9 781738 108824